This Book Belongs To

Orville The Bumble Bee

Who Didn't Believe He Could Fly

Don Haselrig, Author
Judy L. Emerick, Illustrator

Learn Dream Grow Books

GMD Publishing, LLC Pittsburgh, Pennsylvania

To my parents,
Don and Berta
for a lifetime of love and guidance.
To my children, Allen, Danielle and Celeste
who are my greatest sources of love and inspiration.
To my Aunt Jesse for her love and support. --- D.H.

To My Family...
The Loves Of My Life.
Remember to Believe. ---J.L.E

One day,
Orville the bumble bee
was out walking in the forest
when he stopped
in front of a tree.

Orville said to the tree,
"You're so tall.
What can you see?"

The tree said to Orville the bumble bee,
"Come fly up here with me.
Then you shall see."

But slowly and sadly Orville flapped his wings, and said to the tree, "I am a big bumble bee as you can see. Do you really think these little wings of mine will let me fly that high?"

"Why, sure." said the tree to Orville the bumble bee. "Just believe in yourself, and give it a try."

But Orville shook his head and said,
"If I was really made to fly, I would have bigger wings
that would lift me up high into the sky.

But look at these little wings on my back.
I don't believe I can fly, not an inch and not a mile.
I need to keep walking to get my work done.
I must climb flower to flower while I still have the sun."

And so Orville the bumble bee walked on,
but soon grew tired and took a break at a nearby lake.

Just when he stopped, a duck landed on the lake. Orville looked at the duck and said, "Oh, how I wish I had big wings like yours. Then I could fly as high as I wanted, and fast across the sky.

Zug, zug, zug,
I would get my work done,
and then I would fly just to have fun."

The duck said to Orville,
"It is true your wings are perhaps a bit small.
But wings they are, and made to fly. Get them going.
Just give it a try."

But Orville just thought, with a body so big and wings so small, how could they lift him up at all? He said, "I don't believe that I can fly, not an inch and not a mile.

I better keep walking to get my work done. I have much to do while I still have the sun."

Orville
walked past a tree
and a log on the ground.
He huffed and he puffed, and couldn't go on.
He thought about what he was told.
Should he give it a try?
But one look at his little wings
and he couldn't see why.

He just didn't believe they could lift him off the ground, to do his work quickly, then fly all around.

Then he heard a gentle voice from above in the tree.
It spoke to Orville softly,
"Don't you know? Can't you see?"

Orville looked up, as the voice spoke again.
The wise old owl said, "You must listen, my friend."

"You are special as you are, and your little wings are true.
You can fly. You can soar. It is all up to you.

Believe in yourself,
and you can do many things.
Never give up. Give it your best. That, my friend,
is the real test. You were not made to walk.
You were made to fly, and chances are
you can fly very high."

Orville was ready,
and his new friends knew why.
His wings began buzzing
with a big hardy try.

For the first time Orville believed,
and he suddenly found his legs all dangling
with toes off the ground.

Up, up, into the sky
Orville the bumble bee was flying high.
He could see all the flowers
blooming under the sun,
and zug, zug, zug,
he got all his work done.
Then he twirled and looped,
flying just to have fun.

Something had changed in him,
through and through.
Orville learned to believe in himself
and he knew it made all the difference.
He could fly with the little wings on his back.

Now everyone who sees a bumble bee remembers
Orville the bumble bee, who didn't believe he could fly.
Thanks to Orville, we know, if you are different or
if you don't have what others have, you are still special
just the way you are.

Believe in yourself.
Always give your best with a big hardy try,
and just like Orville with his little wings,
you too can do some very special things!

Orville the Bumble Bee
is a Learn Dream Grow children's book series.
Please look for our upcoming books.

Orville The Bumble Bee Makes A Big Discovery.
Orville The Bumble Bee Has A Big Dream.
Orville The Bumble Bee Shares Something With A Friend.